WARNING!

This book
contains nothing
but bad stories,
bad drawings,
bad poems,
bad cartoons,
and bad riddles
about bad characters
doing bad things.
It is a

BAD

book.

ALSO BY ANDY GRIFFITHS
AND ILLUSTRATED BY TERRY DENTON

Just Tricking!
Just Annoying!
Just Stupid!
Just Crazy!
Just Disgusting!
Just Shocking!
Just Macbeth!
Just Doomed!
The Bad Book
The Very Bad Book
The Cat on the Mat is Flat
The Big Fat Cow That Goes Kapow
What Bumosaur is That?
Once upon a Slime
What Body Part is That?
The 13-Storey Treehouse
The 26-Storey Treehouse
The 39-Storey Treehouse
The 52-Storey Treehouse

ALSO BY ANDY GRIFFITHS

The Day My Bum Went Psycho
Zombie Bums from Uranus
Bumageddon: The Final Pongflict

Schooling Around:

Treasure Fever!
Pencil of Doom!
Mascot Madness!
Robot Riot!

the Bad Book

Andy Griffiths
terry Denton

Pan Macmillan Australia

First published 2004 in Pan by Pan Macmillan Australia Pty Limited
1 Market Street, Sydney

Reprinted 2004 (twice), 2006, 2007 (twice), 2008, 2009, 2010 (twice), 2011, 2012 (twice), 2013, 2014 (twice)

National Library of Australia
Cataloguing-in-Publication data:

Griffiths, Andy, 1961–.
The bad book.

For children.
ISBN 978 0 330 36500 0

I. Denton, Terry, 1950–. II. Title

A823.3

Typeset in Jenson 14/18 by Liz Seymour, Seymour Designs
Printed in Australia by McPherson's Printing Group

Papers used by Pan Macmillan Australia Pty Ltd are natural, recyclable products made from wood grown in sustainable forests. The manufacturing processes conform to the environmental regulations of the country of origin.

Contents

Bad Jack Horner

Bad Jack Horner
    Sat in a corner
Pulling the wings off a fly.
    He swore at his mum,
    Kicked his dad in the bum
And said, 'Oh, what a bad boy am I!'

Bad Humpty Dumpty

Humpty Dumpty spray-painted the wall
He covered it with his offensive scrawl.
All the King's horses and all the King's men
Confiscated his spray-can
    and smashed his head in.

Bad Diddle Diddle

Bad diddle diddle
    The cat did a piddle
The cow did a poo on the moon.
    The little dog barfed to see such fun
        And then ate it all up with a spoon.

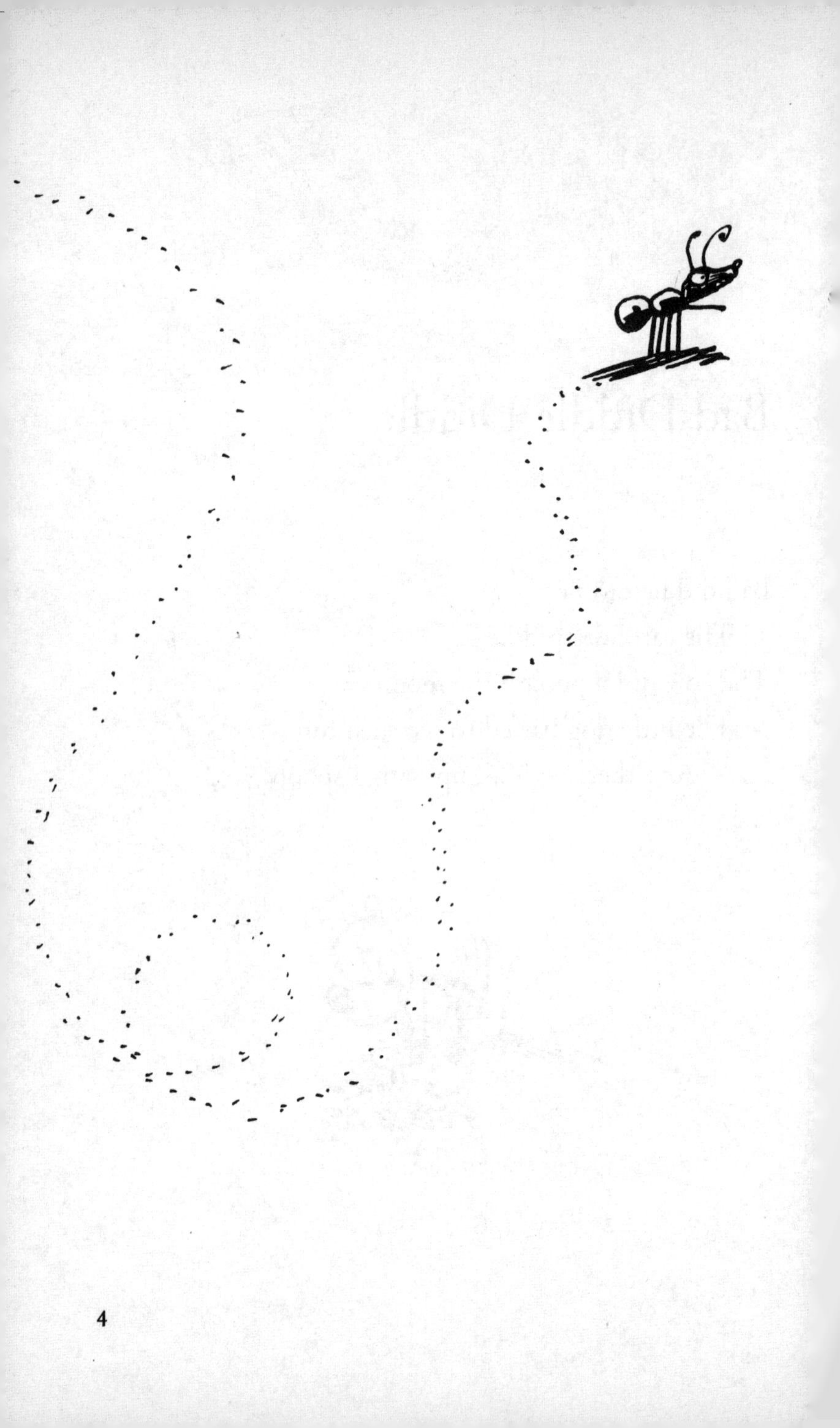

The Bad Ant

Once upon a time there was an ant. It looked like an ordinary ant, but it wasn't. It was a bad ant.

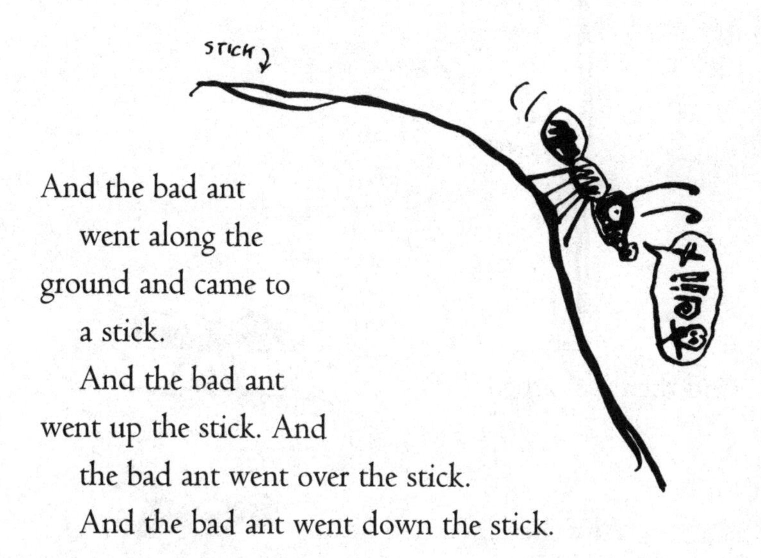

And the bad ant
went along the
ground and came to
a stick.
And the bad ant
went up the stick. And
the bad ant went over the stick.
And the bad ant went down the stick.

And the bad ant went along the ground and came to a bit of grass. And the bad ant went up the bit of grass. And the bad ant went over the bit of grass. And the bad ant went down the bit of grass.

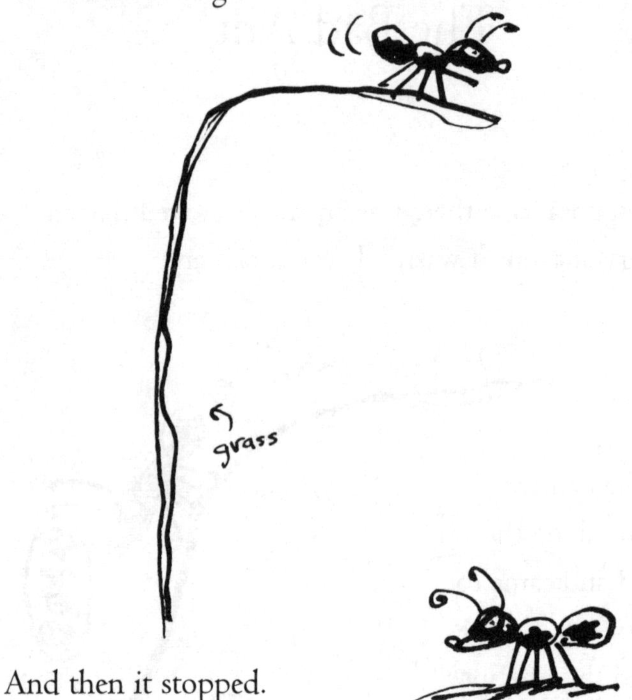

And then it stopped.

And then it started again.

And the bad ant went to Las Vegas,

won ten million dollars

and bought a red sportscar.

And the bad ant
left Las Vegas
and came to a stick.
And the bad ant drove up the stick.
And the bad ant drove over the stick.
And the bad ant drove down the stick.

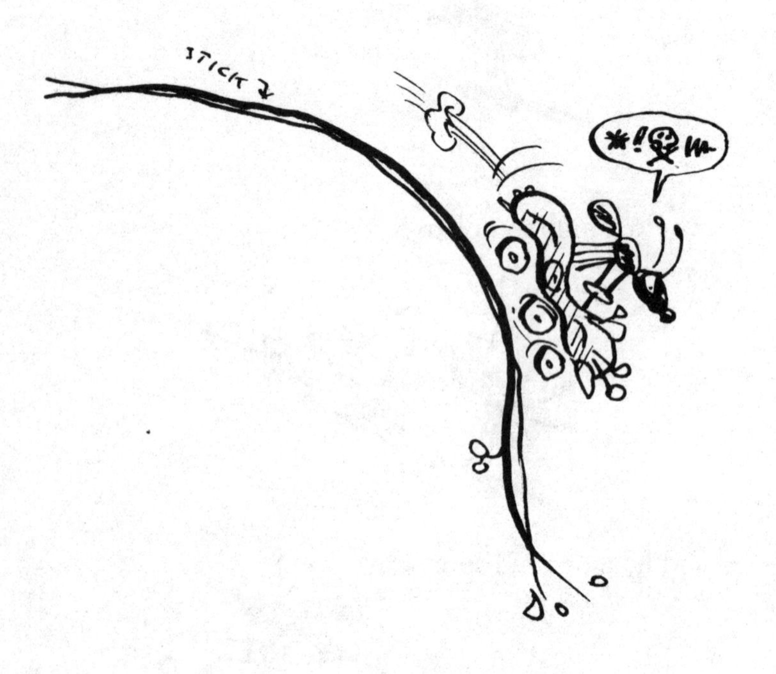

And the bad ant went along the ground
and came to a pedestrian crossing
and saw an old lady who had fallen over.

And the bad ant drove up the old lady.
And the bad ant drove over the old lady.
And the bad ant drove down the old lady.

And just as the bad ant was about to drive off along the road again, it heard the old lady cry out for help. And the bad ant turned around and drove back to the old lady, drove up the old lady and did wheelies on her head. Which wasn't very nice. But not really surprising, because it was a bad ant. A very bad ant.

THE END

Joan Purst

There was a loud girl named Joan Purst
Who always yelled and cursed.
She'd curse and she'd yell
As loud as all hell,
Until everyone's eardrums were burst.

Greedy Little Grace

There was a greedy little girl
Called Greedy Little Grace
Who liked to shovel food non-stop
Into her greedy face.

Her parents said, 'Oh Gracie dear,
Must you eat like that?'
But Greedy Little Grace just laughed
And ate the family cat.

Her mother cried, 'My lovely cat!
I'm really going to miss her!'
But Greedy Little Grace just burped
And ate her little sister.

Her father yelled, 'This gluttony
is not good for your health!'
But Greedy Grace just licked her lips
And then she ate herself.

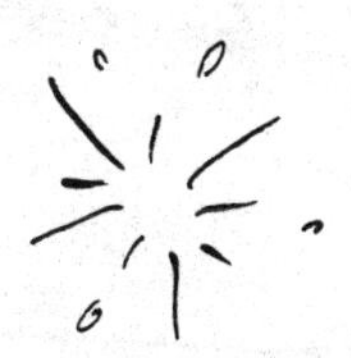

Bad Daddy and the Big Swing

Higher!
Okay.

Higher!
Okay.

Higher!
Okay.

AAARRGGHH!
Uh-oh.

THE END

Badtown

Once upon a time
there was a bad town
called Badtown.

Everybody

who lived in Badtown

was bad-tempered,

had bad breath

and bad luck.

Badtown
suffered non-stop bad weather,
the apple trees of Badtown bore nothing
but bad apples,
and the Badtown newspaper
printed nothing but bad news.

The Badtown national anthem
was full of bad words,

Badtown's national animal was
a badger,

and the national sport
was badminton.

In fact, it was
a game of badminton
that eventually brought the town
to a bad end.

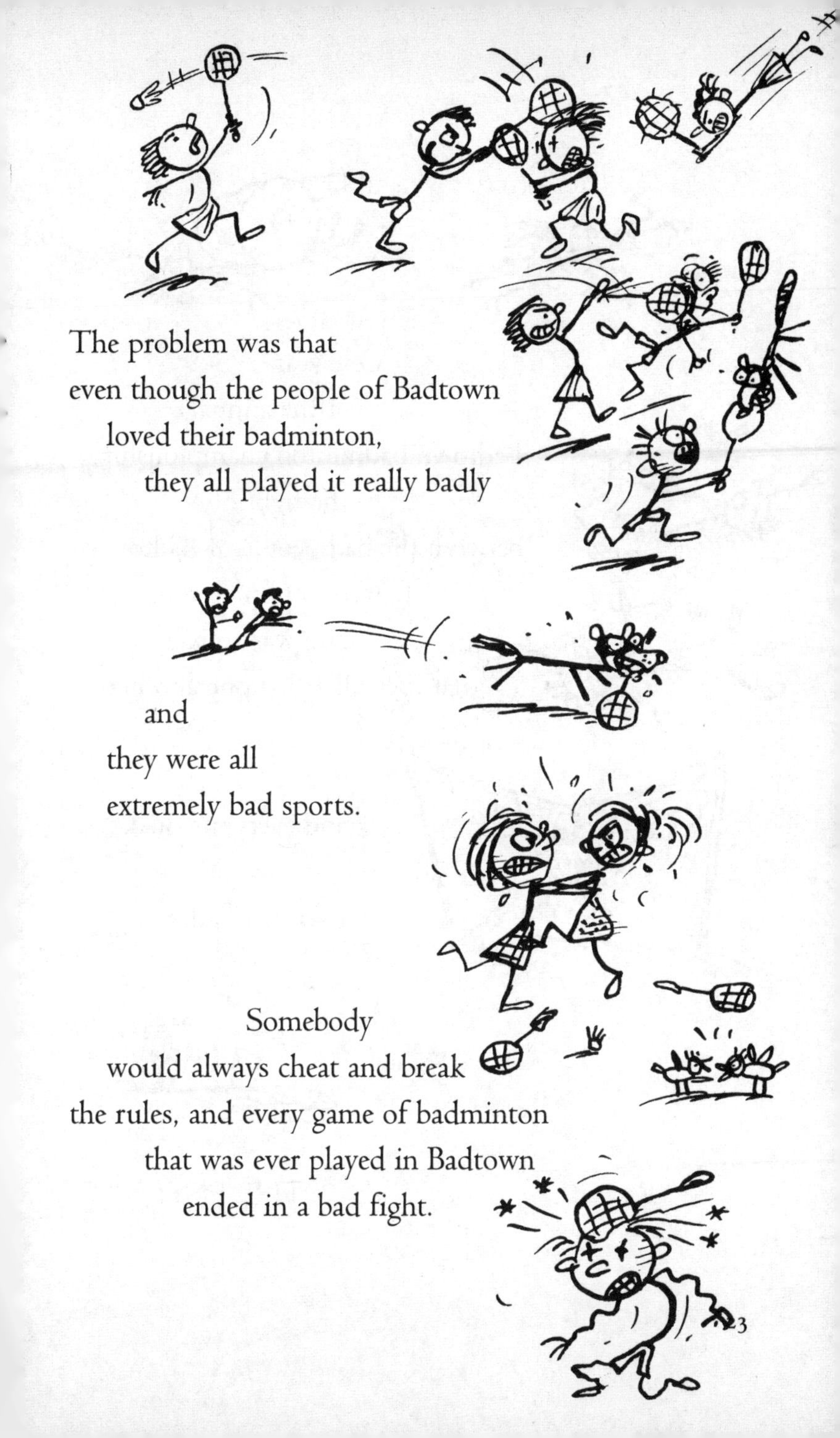

The problem was that
even though the people of Badtown
loved their badminton,
they all played it really badly

and
they were all
extremely bad sports.

Somebody
would always cheat and break
the rules, and every game of badminton
that was ever played in Badtown
ended in a bad fight.

One year
at the annual
Badtown badminton championships,
the fighting
between the bad people of Badtown
went on for so long
and was so bad
that they all killed one another

and everyone died.

Even the badgers.

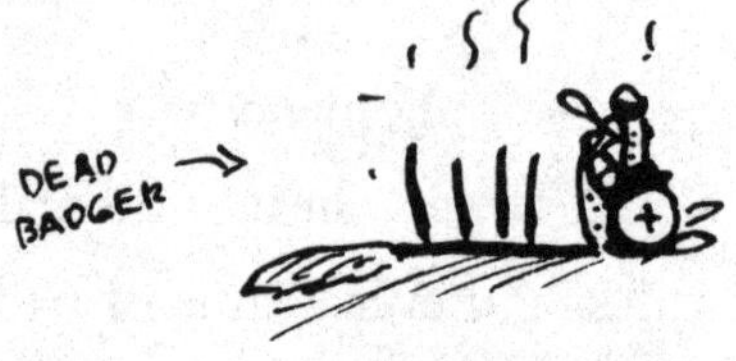

THE END

The Old Lady Who Swallowed a Poo

There was
an old lady
who swallowed a poo.
I don't know why she
    swallowed that poo,
Perhaps
she'll spew.

There was
an old lady
who swallowed a dunny,
That flushed
    and gushed
        and made her smell funny.
She swallowed the dunny to catch the poo.
I don't know why she
    swallowed that poo,
Perhaps
she'll spew.

There was
an old lady
who swallowed a plumber;
Could you get
any dumber than
to swallow
a plumber?

She swallowed the plumber to fix the
dunny,
That flushed
and gushed
and made her smell funny.
She swallowed the dunny to catch the poo.
I don't know why she
swallowed that poo,
Perhaps
she'll spew.

There was
an old lady
who burped with great force—
She spewed
of course.

The Girl Who Slammed Doors

There once was a girl who slammed doors
From morning to night without pause.
  She slammed them so hard
  That the rooms fell apart,
And all that was left were the floors.

Bad Riddles

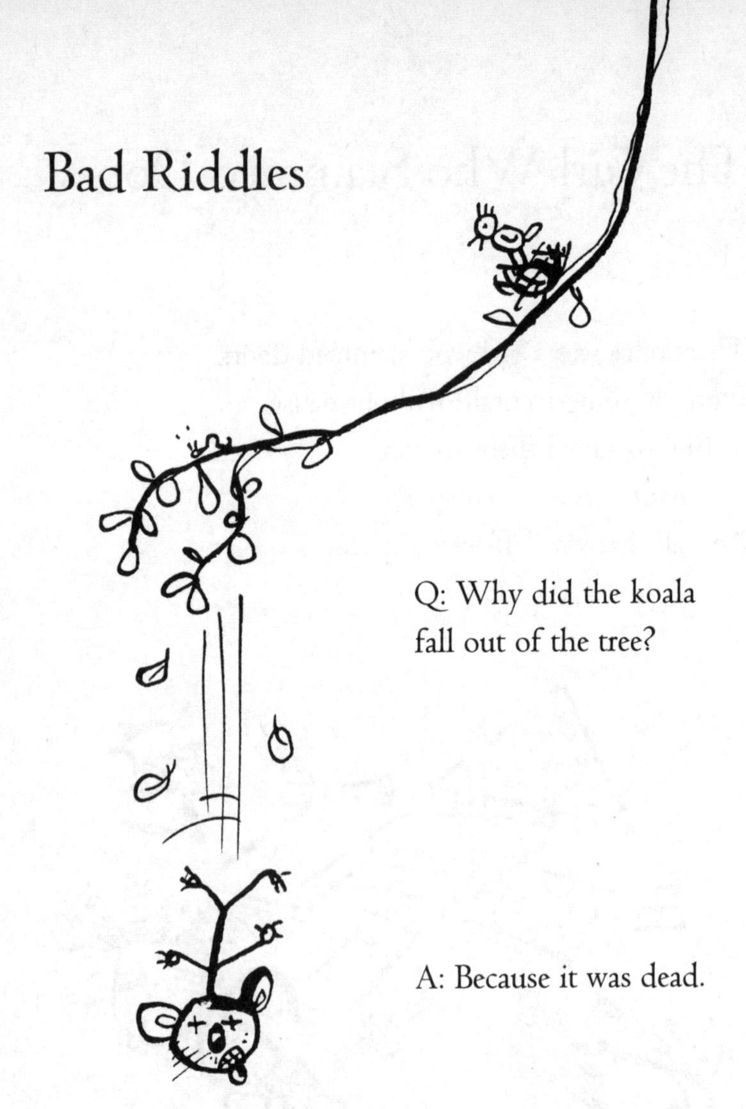

Q: Why did the koala fall out of the tree?

A: Because it was dead.

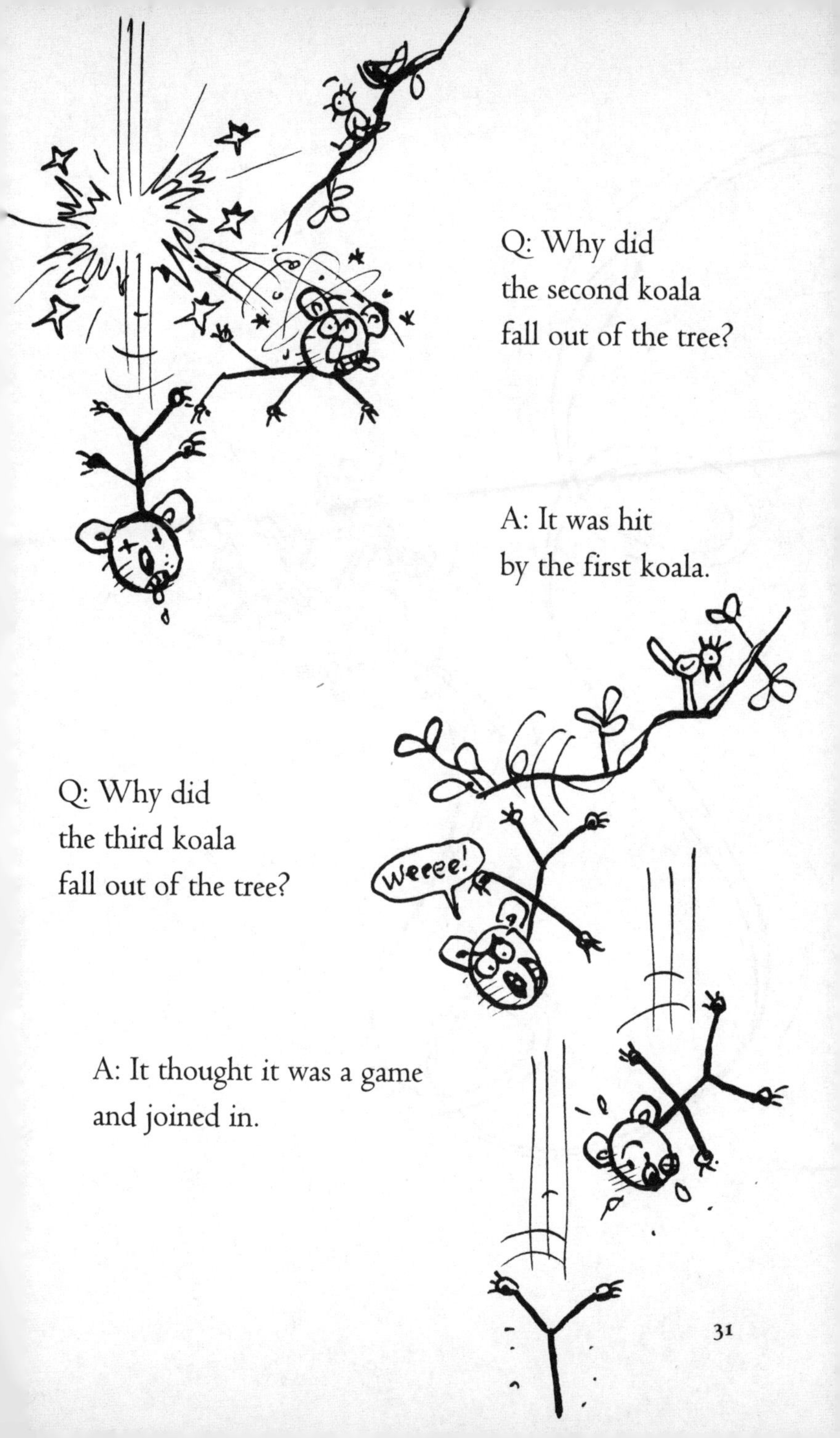

Q: Why did
the second koala
fall out of the tree?

A: It was hit
by the first koala.

Q: Why did
the third koala
fall out of the tree?

A: It thought it was a game
and joined in.

The Sad Bad Bad-man

Once upon a time
          there was a sad bad bad-man.
The sad bad bad-man was sad
               because he was bad
                    at being bad.

So the sad bad bad-man
went to sad bad bad-man's school

where they taught
sad bad bad-men
how to be good at being
good bad-men
instead of being good at being
sad bad bad-men.

And the sad bad bad-man stopped being sad
    and became glad
because he learned how to be a good bad-man
    who was good at being bad
    instead of bad at being bad.

In fact

the ex-sad bad bad-man

was so good at being bad

that he became

the gladdest ex-sad bad bad-man

in the history of

sad bad bad-men

who stopped being sad bad bad-men

and became

glad good bad-men.

THE END

Little Willy

Little Willy took a match
And set fire to his knee.
Said Little Willy as it burnt,
'Ouch, that's hurting me.'

Little Willy took a match
And set fire to his bum.
Said Little Willy as it burnt,
'Gee, that was pretty dumb.'

Little Willy took a match
And set fire to his head.
Said Little Willy as it burnt,
'Soon I will be dead.'

Jeff Pest

There once was a boy called Jeff Pest
Who from being a pest took no rest.
His mother, Celeste,
Said: 'Jeff, without jest,
At being a pest you're the best!'

Bad Mummy and the Very Busy Six-lane Highway

Hmmm…
Pretty please?
All right, but be careful.
YAY! Say 'ready, set, go'!
TRUCK

READY,
SET,
GO!

SCREECH!

SLAM!

CRASH!

THE END

Penny McRose

Penny McRose picked her nose
Morning, noon and night.
She picked it until her head caved in
And her family died of fright.

Bad Terence

One day Mama said, 'Terence dear,
    I must go out and leave you here.
But mind now, Terence, what I say,
        Don't be bad
            while I'm away.'

Terence smiled angelically:
'Fear not, Mama,
you can count on me!'
But Mama had scarcely turned to go
when Terence's eyes
began
to glow...

He pulled a fork out of his pocket,
And stuck it in
an electric socket.
He flicked the switch
and with mighty jolts
Received two hundred and forty volts!

Next
he climbed up on the roof
And—can you believe it?—
What a goof!
He spread his arms out really wide
Jumped off and flapped and…
well… almost flied.

He landed head-first with a crunch
He lost his pride! He lost his lunch!
He shook his head at what he'd done,
Then stumbled inside in search of more fun.

He pulled
his sister's doll
    apart
And stomped upon its tiny heart.
    Then he spied
        the goldfish bowl
    And filled it up
        with cooking oil.

He lit a match
and with a BOOM!
Flaming goldfish filled the room!
Up they flew, higher and higher,
Then down they came
—and set Terence on fire!

He quickly shed his burning clothes
Till he was nude from head to toes.
He wiggled his bum and danced about—
'I love it,' said Terence, 'when Mama goes out!'

Then Mama came home and loudly gasped—
The doll!
The fish!
The oily blast!
And to top it off,
there Terence danced
Not even wearing
underpants!

Mama could not believe her eyes
At this devil in Terence-disguise.
She shook her head
and creased her brow,
'Right!' she said.
'You've done it now!'

Terence squealed and in great haste
    Ran from the room, but Mama gave chase!
Into the bathroom Terence sprinted
    And slammed the door so hard it splintered.

Mama pounded on the door.
        'Come out!' she cried
                in a mighty roar.
Terence looked around frantically
        And then he saw...
                the lavatory!

Now, to flush one's self down the loo
is a very stupid thing to do.
But Terence broke
this simple rule:
Oh naughty boy!
Oh silly fool!

He jumped in,
pushed full flush.
And was swept away
in a mighty gush.
Around the S-bend, down the drain
never to be seen again.

When Mama heard the fatal flush

Many tears
from her eyes did rush.

But they soon dried up
and she felt quite glad

To be rid of a boy
who was so bad.

Bad Baby

CRASH!
NOT THE CAT!
PUT YOUR NAPPY BACK ON!
PLOP!

?
PUT THE PIN BACK IN THAT HAND GRENADE, THIS INSTANT!

THE END

Silly Billy

Silly Billy took a spade
And dug up forty worms,
Then he ate them all alive
Despite the risk of germs.

But pretty soon the silly boy
Began to scream and shout,
Because the worms ate HIM alive
From the inside out.

Very Bad Riddles

Q: Why did the boy fall off his bike?

A: Because his mother threw a fridge at him.

Q: Why did the boy
fail his maths test?

A: Because
his mother
threw a fridge
at him.

Q: Why did the boy suffer multiple fractures, internal bleeding, crushed vertebrae, ruptured organs, brain damage, massive bruising and a sore thumb?

A: Because
he was hit by a truck.

The Bad Little Boy, His Father and the Very Tall Mountain

Once
upon a time
a bad little boy
and his father
climbed
to the top of
a very tall mountain.

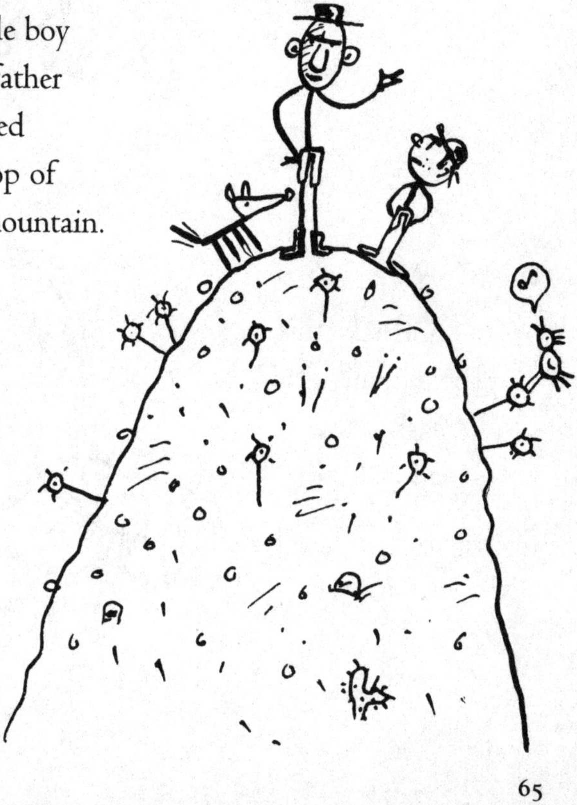

Just as they were about
to climb back down,
the bad little boy
picked up
a pebble.

'Can I take this
pebble home, Dad?'
asked the
bad little boy.

'No, son,' said the father.

'But why not?'
asked the bad little boy.
'It's just one pebble.'

The father smiled.
'That may be true, son,'
he said,
'but if every little boy
who climbed up a mountain
took one pebble home
then there wouldn't be any
mountains left to climb, would there?'

The bad little boy nodded thoughtfully as he considered his father's words.

He pulled a pocket calculator
out of his jacket
and
roughly
calculated how
many billions of pebbles
there were
lying on top
of all the
mountains
on Earth.

Then he calculated how many other
billions and billions
of other pebbles
were hidden inside
the mountains themselves.

The bad little boy
then calculated
how long it would take
for billions and billions
of bad little boys like himself
to remove
all these billions and billions
of pebbles—one by one—before every
mountain on Earth completely disappeared.

When he
had finished
these calculations,
the bad little boy
then considered the complex
practical problem of exactly
how and where all these billions
and billions of bad little boys would store
all these billions and billions of pebbles
in order to avoid forming new mountains consisting
of stolen pebbles.

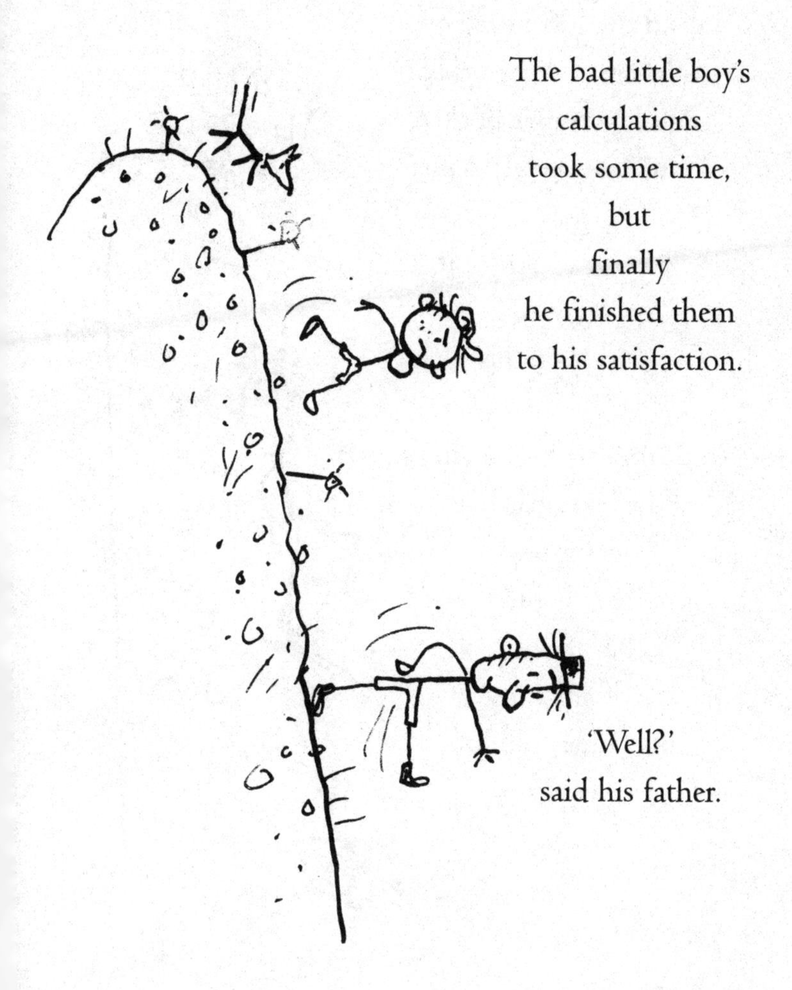

The bad little boy's
calculations
took some time,
but
finally
he finished them
to his satisfaction.

'Well?'
said his father.

'You're right, Dad,'
said the bad little boy
as he slipped the pebble
into his trouser pocket.
'You're absolutely right.'

'I knew you'd see it
my way,'
said his father.

And from that moment on,
the bad little boy
never took
the slightest
bit of notice
of anything
his father told him
ever again.

THE END

Bad Little Betty

Bad little Betty
Wouldn't get out of bed.
Was she being lazy?
No. She was dead.

Bad Daddy Says 'No'

Daddy, can I go here?
No.

Daddy, can I go there?
No.

Daddy, can I breathe in?
No.
Daddy, can I breathe out?
NO!

THE END

Little Snotty Steve

There was a little snotty boy
    Called Little Snotty Steve,
Who liked to wipe his snotty nose
    Upon his snotty sleeve.

    His parents sighed—
        —his parents cried
And politely asked him not to.
    But Little Snotty Steve just sneezed
        And covered them in snot, too.

Bad Baby's Christmas

NOT THE
NATIVITY SCENE!
NOT
GRANDMA!

NOT GRANDPA!
NO, NOT SANTA!
Milk and biscuits
TOYS

THE END

Ruth Punny

There was a rude girl called Ruth Punny
Who thought non-stop burping was funny.
    But one day in the yard
    She burped a little too hard,
And the burp came out all wet and runny.

Pirates, Trucks, Bombs, Sharks, Dinosaurs and Football

Once upon a time there was a bad pirate.

The bad pirate drove around in an old truck,
which had huge black wheels,
a sixteen million fish-power engine
and a whole load of bombs in the back.

The pirate had a pet white pointer shark
that rode on the front of his truck.
If the pirate took a dislike to somebody
—which happened all the time—
the pirate would
throw bombs at them,
and if that didn't work,
the pirate would say
'KILL!'
and the shark
would leap
off the truck
and bite
them
in half.
And that
was pretty much
the pirate's life—
just driving around
throwing bombs and ordering shark attacks
on the unfortunate townspeople and, every
now and then, capturing a ship and stealing all the
chocolate.

But one day the pirate and the shark heard a loud roaring noise.

A huge
dinosaur was
charging
up the road
towards
them!

It had
big sharp claws.

It had
big sharp feet.

It had big sharp blood-dripping teeth.

But the pirate just smiled,
grabbed some bombs
from the back of the truck
and threw them at the dinosaur.

The first bomb
blew off its legs.

The second bomb
blew off its arms.

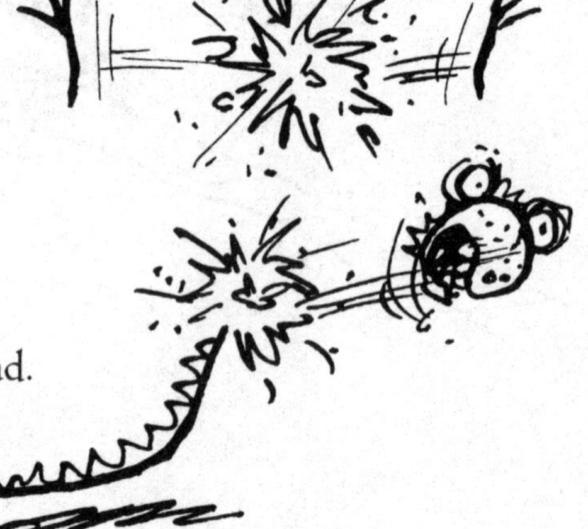

The third bomb
blew off its head.

And the dinosaur—or what was left of it—went crashing down to the ground.

'Good boys,' said the pirate patting the remaining bombs. But while the pirate was doing this,

the dinosaur put its arms back on . . .

and then it put its legs back on . . .

and then it put its head back on.

The pirate heard a loud roaring noise and looked up to see the huge dinosaur once again charging up the road towards the truck. But the pirate just laughed and said to the shark, '*KILL!*'

The terrifying shark launched itself off
the bonnet of the truck,
flew through the air
and bit the dinosaur's heart right
out of its chest.

Then
the shark
bit off its legs.

Then
the shark
bit off its arms.

Then
the shark
bit off
the dinosaur's
head.

And the dinosaur
—or what was left of it—
went crashing down to the ground.

'Good shark,' said the pirate, patting the shark's head. But while the pirate was doing this

the dinosaur put
its arms back on ...
then it put
its legs back on ...

and then it put
its head back on.

This time the pirate
didn't smile
OR laugh.

The bombs hadn't worked.

The shark hadn't worked.

The dinosaur was indestructible!

The dinosaur stood above
the pirate's truck,
and
opened
its
jaws
wide.

But then a curious thing happened.
Instead of swallowing the pirate,
the truck and the shark whole,
it said,
'Hey, wanna
play football?'

The pirate said,
'Sure, but I don't have a football.'
And the
dinosaur said,
'No problem, we can use the shark!'

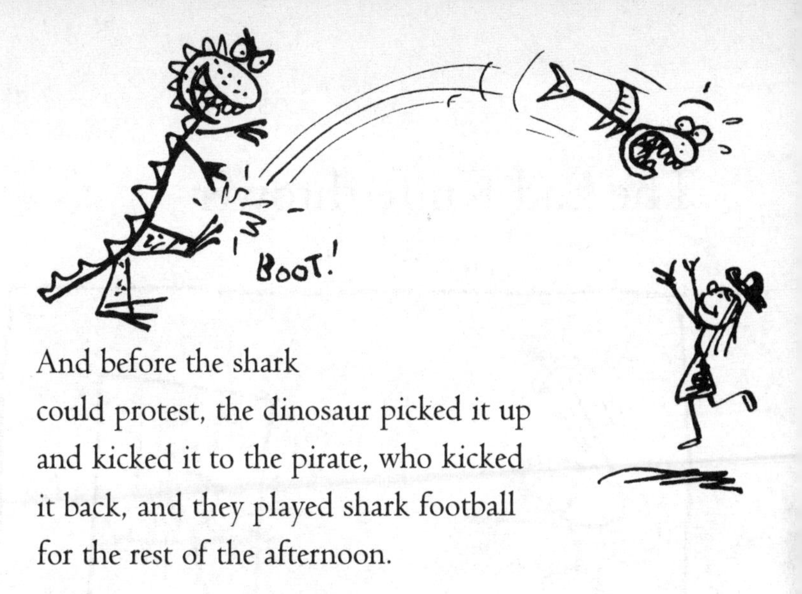

And before the shark
could protest, the dinosaur picked it up
and kicked it to the pirate, who kicked
it back, and they played shark football
for the rest of the afternoon.

And
after dinner
they raced each other
in their trucks until it was time for bed.

THE END

The Bad Knife-thrower

THE END

The Girl
Who Asked
Too Many Questions

There once was a girl
who asked her parents too many questions.
'What is this?' she asked.
'Where are we going?
Why are you doing that?'

Her parents tried their best to answer all her questions, but as soon as they did, the little girl just asked more.

'How big is the moon?

Why does the sun shine?

What does an elephant weigh?

Why is a horse bigger than a mouse?

If people made nests, what would they make them out of?'

Her parents said,
'We are tired of all these questions!
Do not ask us any more.'

But the girl kept on asking.

'Why is the sky blue?' she asked.

'Why is grass green?

If a tiger and a lion had a fight,
which one would win?

What makes thunder?
What makes lightning?
Who made the world?
Who am I?
Where did I come from?
Why am I here?
What does it all mean?’

Then her parents said,
'You ask too many questions!
For goodness sakes, shut up!'

But the little girl
did not shut up.
She said,
'Why do I ask too
many questions?
Why do you want
me to shut up?'

This time, however, her parents
did not answer.
They just
picked
the little girl
up
and
dropped her
into a
very deep hole
and, before
she could ask
'Why did you
pick me up
and drop me
into
a very deep hole?',
her parents
filled it in
and ran away.

THE END

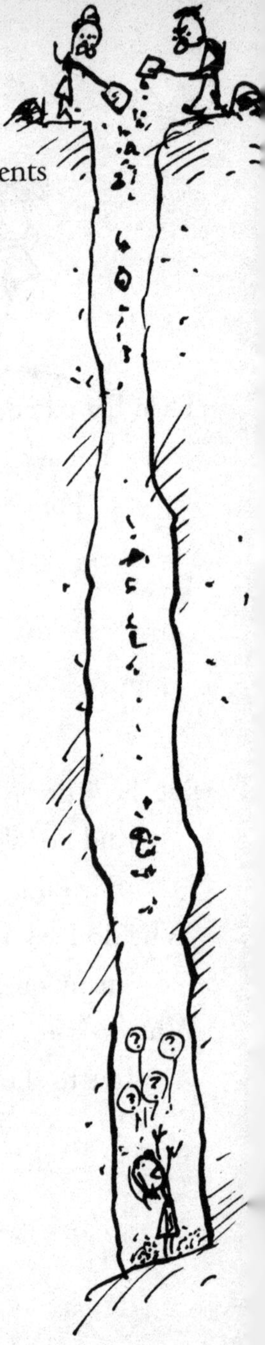

Pete Peddersen

There was a sick boy named
Pete Peddersen
Who refused to take pills
or drink medicine.
With a cough and a splutter,
He fell into a gutter,
And failed to ever get up again.

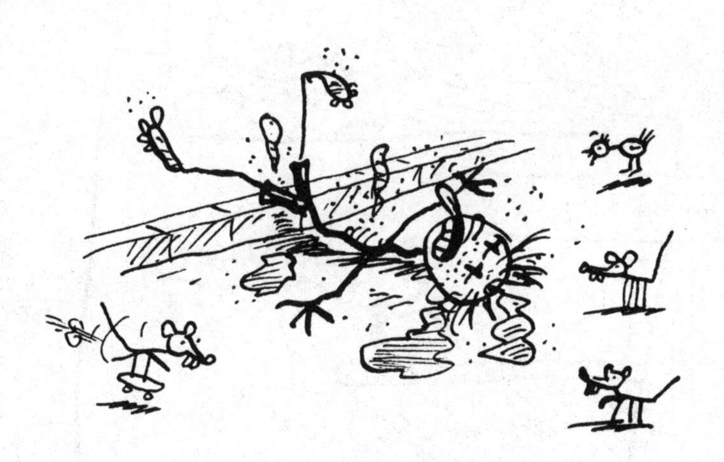

Bad Mummy and the Big Cliff

Hmmm...
Pretty please?
All right, but be careful.
YAY! Say 'ready, set, go'!

READY,
SET,

GO!
Oops…
THE END

The Bad Old Duke of York

Oh, the bad old Duke of York
He had ten thousand men.
He marched them up to the top of the hill,

And pushed them off.

The Bad Granny

Once upon a time there was a bad granny.

She was bad
and evil
and mean.

In fact she was so bad and evil and mean that they put her in a truck with all the other bad grannies and took her to the Granny Smith Apple Factory.

THE END

Little Bad Riding Hood

Once upon a time there was a bad little girl called Little Bad Riding Hood.

One day
her mother said to her,
'Little Bad Riding Hood,
your grandmother is
very sick.

Would you
do me a favour
and take her
this basket of food,
drink
and vital medicine
without which
she will surely die?'

And Little Bad Riding Hood said,

'No.'

THE END

Peter, Peter, Junk-food Eater

Peter, Peter, junk-food eater
Guzzled lemonade by the litre.
Gobbled jelly beans by the tonne
Ate ice-cream cakes and sticky buns.

He began to grow and swell
And was not looking very well.
He drank a milkshake to quench his thirst,
He groaned

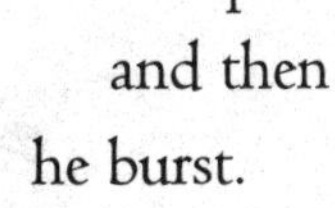

and burped
and then
he burst.

The Bad Builder

Once upon a time
there was a bad builder.

Everybody would say to him
'Can you fix it?'
and he would say,
'No,
I can't.'

THE END

Ed and Ted and Ted's Bad Dog Fred

There was a man
whose name was Ed.
Ed lived in a shed with his friend Ted.

Ted had a bad dog whose name was Fred.

Ed liked Ted and Ted liked Ed
and Fred liked Ted
but he didn't like Ed.

One morning Fred jumped on Ed's bed.
Ed said: 'Fred, get off my bed!'
but Fred just growled
and bit Ed's head.

Ed saw red
and then he said,
'I'm fed up with Fred
always biting my head!
I'm leaving this shed!'

And he went to his car (which was red).
He jumped in and away he fled.

Ted said: 'Ed! Come back to the shed!'
But Ed shook
his head
and sped.

So Ted jumped in his car
(which was also red).

But it wouldn't start.
The battery was dead.

'Bother!

Bother!

Bother!'

said Ted,

'I'll have to take the sled instead.'

He hitched up Fred to the sled,

cracked his whip and

away they sped.

Ted and Fred sped after Ed.

Ted saw Ed's red car up ahead.
'Faster, faster, Fred!' yelled
Ted.

Ted and Fred
were gaining on Ed,
but all of a sudden
Ed stopped dead.
There was
a traffic light.
It was
red!

Ted yelled, 'Fred! Stop the sled!'
But Fred could not.
On they sped.

Ted and Fred smashed into Ed.

Poor Ted and Fred!
They got dead.

Ed hurt his head.
His head bled.

It bled

and bled

and bled

and bled.

His blood was red.

Ed ended up dead like Ted and Fred.

And that was the end
of Ed and Ted
and Ted's bad dog
Fred.

THE END

Very, Very Bad Riddles

Q: Why did the man
cut down the tree?

A: Because it was there.

Q: Why didn't the man cut down the tree?

A: Because it wasn't there.

Q: Why did the tree cut down the man?

A: Because it was a bad tree.

If You're Bad and You Know It

If you're bad and you know it,
pull down your pants,

If you're bad and you know it,
pull down your pants,

If you're bad and you know it,
then you really ought to show it,

If you're bad and you know it,
pull down your pants!

If you're bad and you know it,
say rude words,

If you're bad and you know it,
say rude words,

If you're bad and you know it,
then you really ought to show it,

If you're bad and you know it,
say rude words!

If you're bad and you know it,
blow up the entire universe
and kill every living creature in it,

If you're bad and you know it,
blow up the entire universe
and kill every living creature in it,

If you're bad and you know it,
then you really ought to show it,

If you're bad and you know it,
blow up the entire universe
and kill every living creature in it!

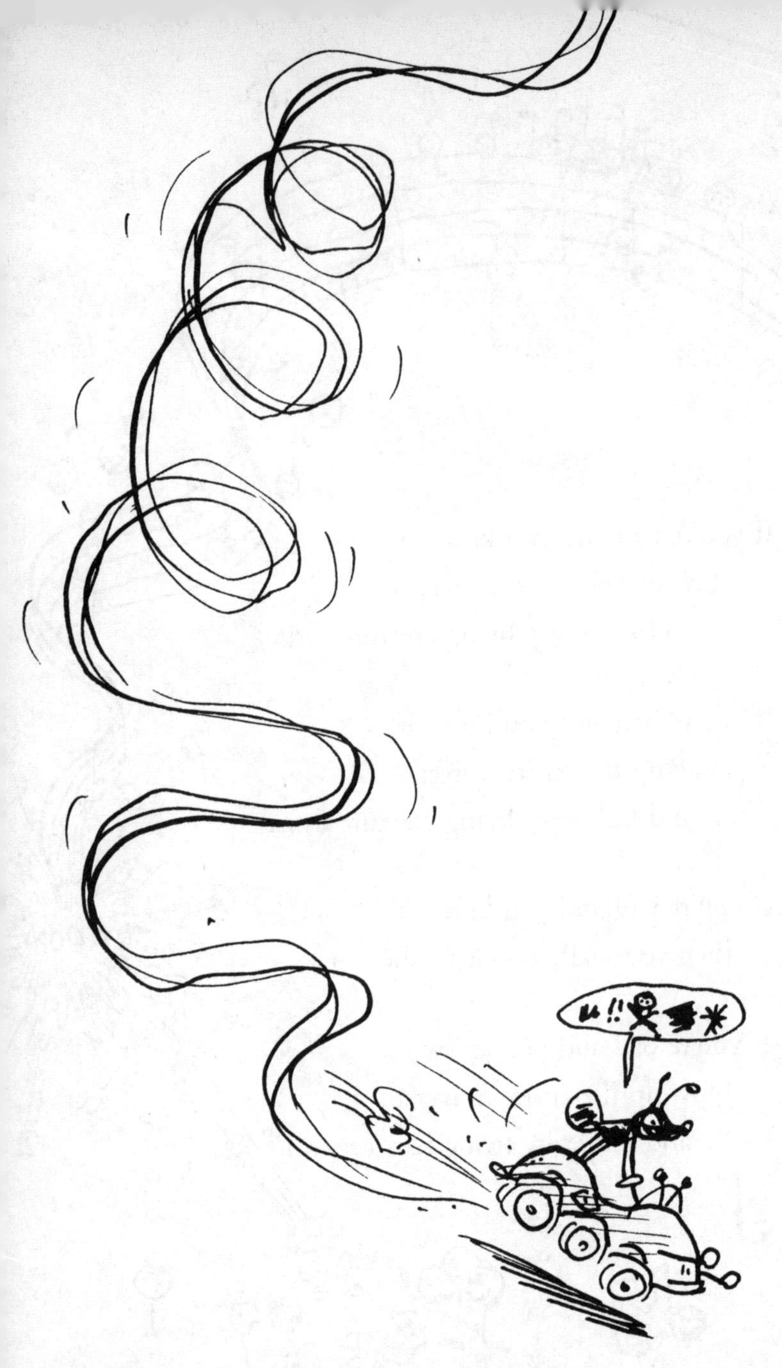

The Day Nothing Bad Happened

One day
nothing bad happened.

Nobody
trod
on their
dog's tail.

Nobody
ran over their cat
with a lawn-mower.

Nobody set themselves on fire.

Nobody
forgot to say
their 'pleases'.

Nobody
forgot to say
their 'thank yous'.

Nobody called anybody 'poo-poo head'.

There were
no hurricanes.

There were
no earthquakes.

There were no
unnecessarily loud burps.

Nothing bad
happened that day.

Nothing bad
at all.

Well,

nothing bad

except for one tiny invasion

of killer cornflakes

from outer space.

But they were quickly neutralised with milk and eaten before the end of the day, with no more harm done than a slightly higher than usual number of people complaining of stomach-ache.

And as the sun
set on the day
that nothing bad happened,
everybody agreed
that it was definitely
the first day in the
history of the Earth
that nothing bad had happened.

Well, nothing *that* bad, anyway.

THE END

Bad Mummy and the Very Hungry Lion

!!
Pretty please?
All right, but be careful.
!!
YAY!

Look, Mummy! He's eating out of my hand!
!!
!
HELP!

THE END

Very, Very, Very Bad Riddles

Q: What's brown and sticky?

A: A stick.

Q: What's yellow and smells like bananas?

A: Monkey vomit.

Q: What's brown and yellow and sticky and smells like bananas?

A: Monkey vomit on a stick.

Bad Baby at the Circus

PUT THOSE DOWN!
COME BACK TO YOUR SEAT THIS INSTANT!

GET DOWN FROM THERE!
GET OFF THAT ELEPHANT ... YOU'LL SQUASH SOME ...

...body
SQUISH!

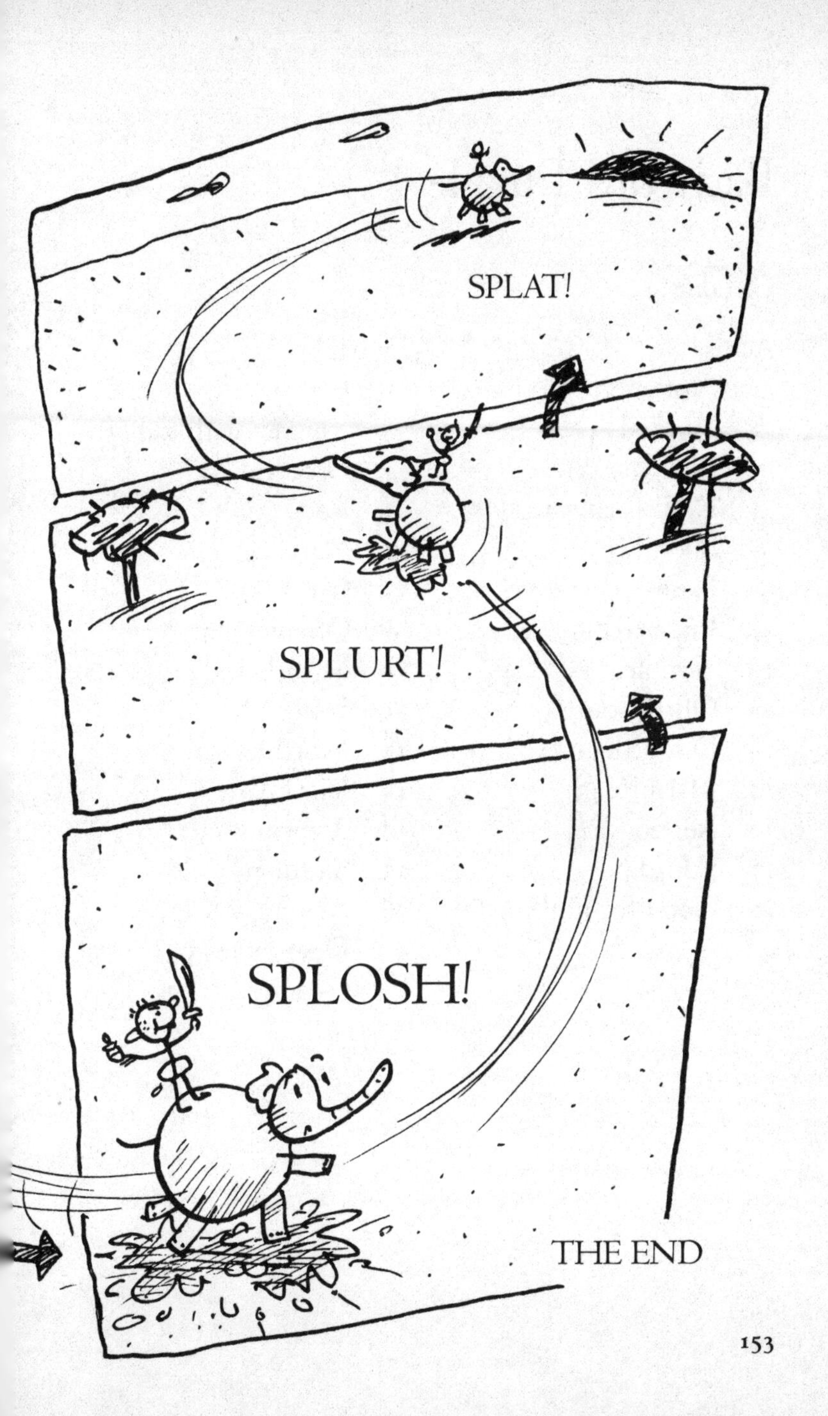
SPLAT!
SPLURT!
SPLOSH!
THE END

Badword Puzzle

CLUES

Across

1. Not good (3)
2. Wicked (3)
3. Naughty (3)
5. DAB backwards (3)
6. Shoddy (3)
8. Faulty (3)
9. Imperfect (3)
10. Terrible (3)
11. Off or sour (3)
13. Disobedient (3)
14. Harmful (3)
16. Rotten (3)
17. Putrid (3)
18. Good-for-nothing (3)

Down

1. Evil (3)
3. Rhymes with sad (3)
4. Dreadful (3)
5. Rude (3)
6. Nasty (3)
7. Gross (3)
8. Offensive (3)
10. Misbehaved (3)
11. Useless (3)
12. Worthless (3)
13. Vile (3)
14. Atrocious (3)
15. Sinful (3)
16. Abominable (3)
17. Despicable (3)

Solution:

The Very Bad Story

Once upon a time things were bad. Then things got very bad. And just when everybody thought things couldn't possibly get any badder, they did.

They got very, very bad.

THE END

The Very, Very Bad Story

Once upon a time things were very, very bad. And just when everybody thought things couldn't possibly get any badder, they did. They got twice as bad.

Then they got three times as bad.

Then they got four thousand, eight hundred and seventy-three and five-sixteenths badder still.

THE END

The Very, Very, Very Bad Story

Once upon a time things were four thousand, eight hundred and seventy-three and five-sixteenths badder than the time things were three times as bad as the time things were twice as bad as the time when they were just very, very bad.

In fact things were SO bad that it made all the previous bad days seem like the good old days and the memory of those good old bad days made everybody cry and feel very sorry for themselves and feel even badder than they already did.

But eventually people started saying, 'Hey, we can't just sit around crying all day and feeling bad. We should try to fix things and make everything good again.'

So everybody got up, wiped their tears away, stopped feeling sorry for themselves and tried to make things good again.

But it was no use. The more they tried to make things good again, the badder things got. Things just got badder and

badder and badder and badder and badder and badder
and badder and badder and badder and badder and
badder and badder and badder and badder and badder
and badder and badder and badder and badder and
badder and badder and badder and badder and badder
and badder and badder and badder and badder and
badder and badder and badder and badder and badder
and badder and badder and badder and badder and
badder and badder and badder and badder and badder
and badder and badder and badder and badder and
badder and badder and badder and badder and badder
and badder and badder and badder and badder and
badder and badder and badder and badder and badder
and badder and badder and badder and badder and
badder and badder and badder and badder and badder
and badder and badder and badder and badder and
badder and badder and badder and badder and badder
and badder and badder and badder and badder and
badder and badder and badder and badder and badder
and badder and badder and badder and badder and
badder and badder and badder and badder and badder
and badder and badder and badder and badder and
badder and badder and badder and badder and badder
and badder and badder and badder and badder and

badder and badder and badder and badder and badder
and badder and badder and badder and badder and
badder and badder and badder and badder and badder
and badder and badder and badder and badder and
badder and badder and badder and badder and badder
and badder and badder and badder and badder and
badder and badder and badder and badder and badder
and badder and badder and badder and badder and
badder and badder and badder and badder and badder
and badder and badder and badder and badder and
badder and badder and badder and badder and badder
and badder and badder and badder and badder and
badder and badder and badder and badder and badder
and badder and badder and badder and badder and
badder and badder and badder and badder and badder
and badder and badder and badder and badder and
badder and badder and badder and badder and badder
and badder and badder and badder and badder and
badder and badder and badder and badder and badder
and badder and badder and badder and badder and
badder and badder and badder and badder and badder
and badder and badder and badder and badder and
badder and badder and badder and badder and badder
and badder and badder and badder and badder and

badder and badder and badder and badder and badder
and badder and badder and badder and badder and
badder and badder and badder and badder and badder
and badder and badder and badder and badder and
badder and badder and badder and badder and badder
and badder and badder and badder and badder and
badder and badder and badder and badder and badder
and badder and badder and badder and badder and
badder and badder and badder and badder and badder
and badder and badder and badder and badder and
badder and badder and badder and badder and badder
and badder and badder and badder and badder and
badder and badder and badder and badder and badder
and badder and badder and badder and badder and
badder and badder and badder and badder and badder
and badder and badder and badder and badder and
badder and badder and badder and badder and badder
and badder and badder and badder and badder and
badder and badder and badder and badder and badder
and badder and badder and badder and badder and
badder and badder and badder and badder and badder
and badder and badder and badder and badder and
badder and badder and badder and badder and badder
and badder and badder and badder and badder and

badder and badder and badder and badder and badder
and badder and badder and badder and badder and
badder and badder and badder and badder and badder
and badder and badder and badder and badder and
badder and badder and badder and badder and badder
and badder and badder and badder and badder and
badder and badder and badder and badder and badder
and badder and badder and badder and badder and
badder and badder and badder and badder and badder
and badder and badder and badder and badder and
badder and badder and badder and badder and badder
and badder and badder and badder and badder and
badder and badder and badder and badder and badder
and badder and badder and badder and badder and
badder and badder and badder and badder and badder
and badder and badder and badder and badder and
badder and badder and badder and badder and badder
and badder and badder and badder and badder and
badder and badder and badder and badder and badder
and badder and badder and badder and badder and
badder and badder and badder and badder and badder
and badder and badder and badder and badder and
badder and badder and badder and badder and badder
and badder and badder and badder and badder and

badder and badder and badder and badder and badder
and badder and badder and badder and badder and
badder and badder and badder and badder and badder
and badder and badder and badder and badder and
badder and badder and badder and badder and badder
and badder and badder and badder and badder and
badder and badder and badder and badder and badder
and badder and badder and badder and badder and
badder and badder and badder and badder and badder
and badder and badder and badder and badder and
badder and badder and badder and badder and badder
and badder and badder and badder and badder and
badder and badder and badder and badder and badder
and badder and badder and badder and badder and
badder and badder and badder and badder and badder
and badder and badder and badder and badder and
badder and badder and badder and badder and badder
and badder and badder and badder and badder and
badder and badder and badder and badder and badder
and badder and badder and badder and badder and
badder and badder and badder and badder and badder
and badder and badder and badder and badder and
badder and badder and badder and badder and badder
and badder and badder and badder and badder and

badder and badder and badder and badder and badder
and badder and badder and badder and badder and
badder and badder and badder and badder and badder
and badder and badder and badder and badder and
badder and badder and badder and badder and badder
and badder and badder and badder and badder and
badder and badder and badder and badder and badder
and badder and badder and badder and badder and
badder and badder and badder and badder and badder
and badder and badder and badder and badder and
badder and badder and badder and badder and badder
and badder and badder and badder and badder and
badder and badder and badder and badder and badder
and badder and badder and badder and badder and
badder and badder and badder and badder and badder
and badder and badder and badder and badder and
badder and badder and badder and badder and badder
and badder and badder and badder and badder and
badder and badder and badder and badder and badder
and badder and badder and badder and badder and
badder and badder and badder and badder and badder
and badder and badder and badder and badder and
badder and badder and badder and badder and badder
and badder and badder and badder and badder and

badder and badder and badder and badder and badder
and badder and badder and badder and badder and
badder and badder and badder and badder and badder
and badder and badder and badder and badder and
badder and badder and badder and badder and badder
and badder and badder and badder and badder and
badder and badder and badder and badder and badder
and badder and badder and badder and badder and
badder and badder and badder and badder and badder
and badder and badder and badder and badder and
badder and badder and badder and badder and badder
and badder and badder and badder and badder and
badder and badder and badder and badder and badder
and badder and badder and badder and badder and
badder and badder and badder and badder and badder
and badder and badder and badder and badder and
badder and badder and badder and badder and badder
and badder and badder and badder and badder and
badder and badder and badder and badder and badder
and badder and badder and badder and badder and
badder and badder and badder and badder and badder
and badder and badder and badder and badder and
badder and badder and badder and badder and badder
and badder and badder and badder and badder and

badder and badder and badder and badder and badder
and badder and badder and badder and badder and
badder and badder and badder and badder and badder
and badder and badder and badder and badder and
badder and badder and badder and badder and badder
and badder and badder and badder and badder and
badder and badder and badder and badder and badder
and badder and badder and badder and badder and
badder and badder and badder and badder and badder
and badder and badder and badder and badder and
badder and badder and badder and badder and badder
and badder and badder and badder and badder and
badder and badder and badder and badder and badder
and badder and badder and badder and badder and
badder and badder and badder and badder and badder
and badder and badder and badder and badder and
badder and badder and badder and badder and badder
and badder and badder and badder and badder and
badder and badder and badder and badder and badder
and badder and badder and badder and badder and
badder and badder and badder and badder and badder
and badder and badder and badder and badder and
badder and badder and badder and badder and badder
and badder and badder and badder and badder and

badder and badder and badder and badder and badder
and badder and badder and badder and badder and
badder and badder and badder and badder and badder
and badder and badder and badder and badder and
badder and badder and badder and badder and badder
and badder and badder and badder and badder and
badder and badder and badder and badder and badder
and badder and badder and badder and badder and
badder and badder and badder and badder and badder
and badder and badder and badder and badder and
badder and badder and badder and badder and badder
and badder and badder and badder and badder and
badder and badder and badder and badder and badder
and badder and badder and badder and badder and
badder and badder and badder and badder and badder
and badder and badder and badder and badder and
badder and badder and badder and badder and badder
and badder and badder and badder and badder and
badder and badder and badder and badder and badder
and badder and badder and badder and badder and
badder and badder and badder and badder and badder
and badder and badder and badder and badder and
badder and badder and badder and badder and badder
and badder and badder and badder and badder and

badder and badder and badder and badder and badder
and badder and badder and badder and badder and
badder and badder and badder and badder and badder
and badder and badder and badder and badder and
badder and badder and badder and badder and badder
and badder and badder and badder and badder and
badder and badder and badder and badder and badder
and badder and badder and badder and badder and
badder and badder and badder and badder and badder
and badder and badder and badder and badder and
badder and badder and badder and badder and badder
and badder and badder and badder and badder and
badder and badder and badder and badder and badder
and badder and badder and badder and badder and
badder and badder and badder and badder and badder
and badder and badder and badder and badder and
badder and badder and badder and badder and badder
and badder and badder and badder and badder and
badder and badder and badder and badder and badder
and badder and badder and badder and badder and
badder and badder and badder and badder and badder
and badder and badder and badder and badder.

THE END